Frankie the Blankie

Jennifer Sattler

BLOOMSBURY
NEW YORK LONDON OXFORD NEW DELHI SYDNEY

First published in the United States of America in May 2016
by Bloomsbury Children's Books
www.bloomsbury.com

Bloomsbury is a registered trademark of Bloomsbury Publishing Plc

For information about permission to reproduce selections from this book, write to
Permissions, Bloomsbury Children's Books, 1385 Broadway, New York, New York 10018
Bloomsbury books may be purchased for business or promotional use. For information on bulk purchases
please contact Macmillan Corporate and Premium Sales Department at specialmarkets@macmillan.com

Library of Congress Cataloging-in-Publication Data
Names: Sattler, Jennifer Gordon, author, illustrator.
Title: Frankie the blankie/by Jennifer Sattler.
Description: New York : Bloomsbury Children's Books, 2016.
Summary: Doris the Gorilla and her blankie, Frankie, do everything together so when a fellow jungle mate suggests blankies are for babies,
Doris tries to give Frankie up, but life without her blanket is just not the same so she disguises it for the other jungle animals.
Identifiers: LCCN 2015037214
ISBN 978-1-61963-675-0 (hardcover) • ISBN 978-1-68119-034-1 (board book)
Subjects: | CYAC: Gorilla—Fiction. | Blankets—Fiction. | Jungle animals—Fiction. | Disguise—Fiction. |
Board books. | BISAC: JUVENILE FICTION / Animals / Apes, Monkeys, etc. |
JUVENILE FICTION / Social Issues / Friendship. | JUVENILE FICTION / Animals / Jungle Animals.
Classification: LCC PZ7.S24935 Fr 2016 | DDC [E]—dc23
LC record available at http://lccn.loc.gov/2015037214

Art created with acrylics and Adobe Photoshop
Typeset in Versailles LT Std
Book design by Yelena Safronova
Printed in China by Leo Paper Products, Heshan, Guangdong
1 3 5 7 9 10 8 6 4 2

All papers used by Bloomsbury Publishing, Inc., are natural, recyclable products made from wood grown in well-managed forests.
The manufacturing processes conform to the environmental regulations of the country of origin.

For Mayzie and her beloved "Blankie,"
who she loved to shreds:

Doris was never alone.
She had her blankie, Frankie.

Frankie was with Doris when she took a nap.

He was with her at snack time.

And he was a very graceful
dance partner.

One day, Doris was having a wonderful time with Frankie.

Until . . .

"Only *babies* play with blankies, *you know.*"

Doris was embarrassed.

But she missed him too much and had a terrible day.

Doris had an idea. She would disguise Frankie.

Later on, she pretended she had a boo-boo.

"I slipped on a banana peel, so I have to wear this bandage. Nothin' special, just a plain old bandage."

Instead, Doris pretended Frankie was just a hankie.
"Oh boy, sure is hot out," she sighed.

ACHOO!

That was close—too close,
thought Doris.

She decided to find a secret place to hide Frankie,
and she would visit him throughout the day.

But one day as she was playing with Frankie in the secret place, Doris felt like she was being watched.

Doris thought for a moment.

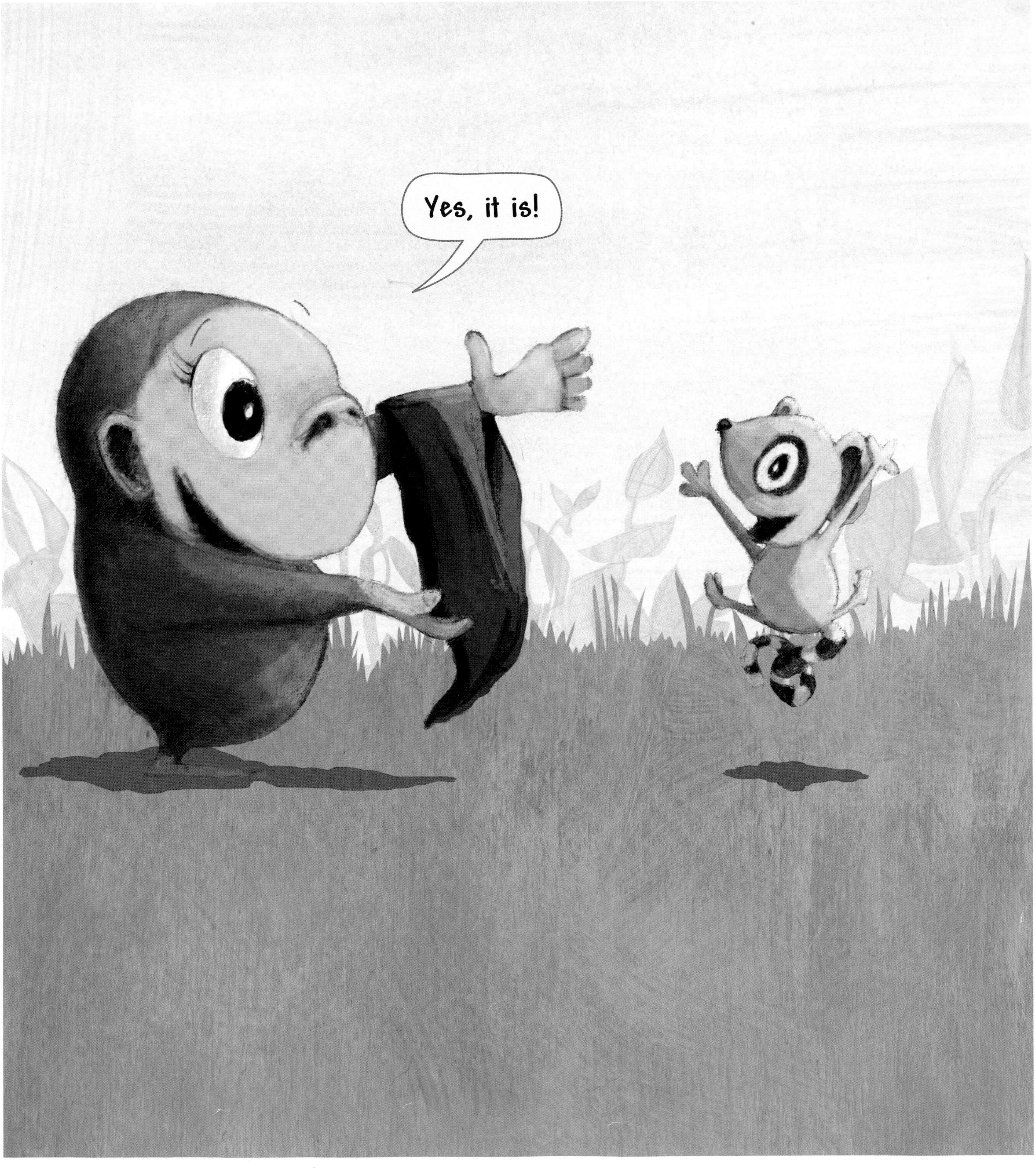
Yes, it is!

Doris and Frankie put on a show.

There was danger!

Laughter!

Love!

And soon . . .

. . . news spread through the jungle
of Doris and her amazing puppet.
Frankie was irresistible!

They just had to get to know him.